OUTHOUSE BLUES

David Dick

David Dick

Illustrations by Jackie Larkins

First Edition, September 2009

Copyright by Plum Lick Publishing, Incorporated
P. O. Box 68, North Middletown, KY 40357-0068
or 1101 Plum Lick Road, Paris, KY 40361

www.plumlickpublishing.com

Dust jacket design and book production
by Stacey Freibert Design
Illustrations by Jackie Larkins
Photograph of David Dick by Chuck Perry

Other books by David Dick

The View from Plum Lick
Peace at the Center
A Conversation with Peter P. Pence
The Quiet Kentuckians
The Scourges of Heaven
Follow the Storm: A Long Way Home
Jesse Stuart — The Heritage
A Journal for Lalie — Living Through Prostate Cancer
Let There Be Light — The Story of Rural Electrification in Kentucky

Books by David and Lalie Dick

Home Sweet Kentucky
Rivers of Kentucky
Kentucky — A State of Mind

ISBN: 978-0-9755037-4-4
Library of Congress Control Number: 2009905876

for Lalie

"Outhouse" is the planet on which we live.
"Blues" is a prayerful conversation in which we try
to explain and hopefully redeem ourselves. The core
of our beings clings doggedly to the
belief that all roads lead to a better home far,
far away.

As I sit here in the outhouse on my eightieth birthday, singing the blues, tootin' and poopin', a lifetime of voices rings in my scrambled brain.

But, what's to be frittered-minded about? Just another bridge over spumy water, one more day with the sun hiding behind winter clouds over Plum Lick, Kentucky. Just another slow and careful walk through the icy backyard, beneath the sorry, old, yellowed pear tree, beyond the Mississippi magnolia and the Kentucky water maples to the outhouse temple, where an out-to-pasture network correspondent no longer has urgent need for radio, television, or the *New York Times*.

My late physician father, Samuel, used to say, "When we lived at Henley's, somebody stole Tinker's gander," which was his favorite retort when dealing with non-earth-shaking events or when bored with nattering conversations. Making his Great Depression rounds of house calls in Cincinnati, fees paid mainly with chickens, eggs, and maybe a hungry pup or two, he counted most idle talk as hardly more than ticks on Grandfather's clock. What on earth do bits of blab matter four billion years after the Big Blam?

As an old network newsman once stated the case for journalism, "We have a vested interest in chaos."

As for weather forecasters, however well-intentioned, they could hardly do without approaching fronts, blue northers, tornadoes, hurricanes, and tsunamis. Meantime, heroic doomsday news merchants feast on train derailments, plane crashes, nightclub fires, earthquakes, volcanic eruptions, and whether or not the First Lady wears sleeves.

"We live in a perfect world with imperfect consequences," Dr. Daddy might have added with his Prohibition-era, laboratory-gin smile. Those were the jazz-age days of "Having a party?" Be sure to invite a medical student! They'll bring the stuff, "Medical student throwing a party? By all means, go!"

As for me, I was rudely awakened in 1993 when with results of my own medical test in hand, the Family Marshal of viruses, skin rashes, and broken bones spoke with most solemn tone on the telephone: "You better come in because something's wrong here."

"I'm 90 percent sure it's cancer," said the next doctor as earnestly as if he were laying into the strings of "Fiddler on the Roof."

"We need to do a bone scan, a biopsy, then exploratory surgery to see if the cancer cells have made the jump to the landing pads of the lymph nodes. While you're on the table we'll send pathology samples to the lab. Depending on the results we'll decide where to go from there."

"Oh, my Lord," I murmured from the depths of my outhouse lower region, down where the colon, kidneys, bladder, urinary racetrack, prostate lump, little boy things, and foreshortened tally-whimper hang around sometimes helter-skelter. My bell had been rung. Loud and clear. Jumping frogs in the middle of the night landing on innocent lily pads. Say it ain't so, Doc.

The walls of the outhouse cried out for restitution. I began to sing the blues. My mind returned to the days when I would howl with a half-breed hound named Blue. He was deeply concerned about my distress.

"Why in the name of God's outhouses did you wait so long to have a checkup?" said the look in Blue's doleful eyes.

Why did God make so many males so *Sturm und Drang*? Why did he make most dogs so willing to follow their masters to Kingdom Come?

"Stupid! Just plain down and dirty stupid," I replied.

"Man-dog thing," Blue muttered as we revved up another round of howling.

Outhouses, talking dogs, and some fortunate blues singers are known for cockeyed optimism. This was duly noted when the news emerged from the operating room with its bright lights, masked faces, nimble, well-scrubbed fingers, and hushed voices (except for understandable gallows guffaws—His name is Mr. Dick).

No lymph node jumps! Bone scan negative!

I was sewed up and scheduled for radiation—nuclear medicine, they call it.

As luck would have it, a year or two later the surgeon took retirement. But before he departed, I asked him the big one—"How long do I have to live, Doctor?"

"About ten years."

On the outhouse clock, that was about fifteen years ago.

My forecaster of probabilities was replaced by another specialist. "The die is cast," he said as unflinchingly as a Las Vegas croupier. But, damn it all, I wasn't in this for craps in anybody's outhouse,

and I told him I was getting myself another doctor.

Ten years after the die was thrown,
"You have one to two years to live, *with*
chemo" said the fourth doctor after hor-
monal therapy that left me impotent and
incontinent. This was followed by a dou-
ble orchiectomy (removal of both of the
little boy things that feed the testosterone
fire, which in turn make the prostate
very angry). In outhouse time, this was
about three years ago. I haven't stopped
singing the blues, which probably has
been the best medicine of all.

Hello protective underwear. So long
rowdy Saturday nights and rambling
Sunday mornings. Maybe the Great
Creator was right-on, understandably
concerned that if something were not put
in the way, man might testosterone him-
self to death.

"Just remember, there is no curative,

only a palliative," said the fifth doctor with the chemo needle and wit as dry as a buffalo chip. In other words, I'm going to die, but maybe I can delay the inevitable long enough to go to the outhouse and reminisce about the dogs I've known and loved.

So here I sit, as I say, singing the blues on my eightieth birthday—February 2010—power off and on along the road to Plum Lick because of iced-down lines, and what do I hear but a scratching on the outhouse door?
    "Boss?"
    "Who's out there?"
    "It's me, your old buddy."
    "Cat?"
    "Of course. What are you doing in there?"
    "Whadaya think I'm doing in here besides freezing my butt off?"

"Tootin' and poopin'?"

"More toot than poop."

"Well, are you going to invite in a sweet old Catahoula pup, or not?"

Cat the Catahoula dog was bred to ignore the wild hog's first roaring rush, go

for the ear, and hold on tight—a game hard-charging wild hogs don't like to play. Malignant cells don't think much of it either.

At M.D. Anderson Cancer Center in Houston, Texas, their motto is, "We're Making Cancer History," or, as the dog named Cat would say, "We take the wild hog by the ear and make him sit down."

Two years of chemotherapy at M.D. Anderson with the sixth and seventh doctors have brought my PSA down from nearly 400 to 21.7, and while I may not be poster child for all seasons, which has been suggested by a few smiling nurses, I'm mighty grateful for each and every new sunrise. Each precious moment spent in the rickety old three-holer outhouse when it's sorely needed. When all else fails it's good for the aching soul!

"Come on in," I say, pushing open the palace door, shaking snow from the cold-as-kraut hinges. Cat bounds in and just about knocks me off the center throne of the wasp-launching three-holer. She licks my face with her pink tongue, not missing mouth, nose, or eyes. If I don't say something quick she'll clean out both my ears.

"Cat, for God's sake, go easy."

"Happy birthday to you, happy birthday to you, happy birthday dear Bosssss, happy birthday to you!"

"How in hell did you get here?"

"Walked the five miles from where you left me with your domino-playing neighbors Michael and Miranda. You said you had to find me a new home because of all your travels to see doctors. Said I might get into trouble if I was left to my own wild-hog initiatives. So I said, 'Cat, you're a damn poor excuse for a wild-hog hunter if you don't get your sorry butt over to wish Boss a happy eightieth birthday, even though he did discard you like a dried piece of pork chop.'"

"I'm sorry it worked out that way, Cat. But Miz Scarlett and I gave it a lot of thought. A relocated dog named Cat is better than a dead dog named Whoever."

"O.K. Boss. May I suggest you adjust your protective underwear, put down that silly centerfold, pull up your corduroys, stuff in your L.L. Bean wool shirt, buckle your belt with your name on it so's you can be identified if lost in a February snow storm, and come with me to the house where Miz Scarlett is waiting for her Iditarod idol. I've a little surprise for you. Yes Sir, I sure do."

"She knows you're here?"

"I stopped at the house first. She cried all over me and told me you were up here in the igloo."

"Miz Scarlett has missed you, Cat."

"I know, and I love her."

"There aren't many humans who understand dog talk the way you and I do, Cat. Maybe we can reach them in a small book I'm writing, maybe teach them something straight from the outhouse. Who knows, maybe we can make it easier for Miz Scarlett, my wife, caregiver, and soul mate for the past thirty-six years."

"You wanna teach her to talk to dogs?"

"Why not?"

"True as true can be. Are you ready? Race you to the big house!"

"You and the hog's ear you rode in on."

"Just pullin' your leg."

"For God's sake, don't pull my leg, and take it easy going down the slope to the back door," I say as we gingerly slog through the snow past what used to be the chicken house, meat house, coal house, and ivy-covered wagon wheels.

"Things of the past?" says Cat, sniffing

the terrain.

"Like yours truly."

"You ain't no propped-up wagon wheel, Boss."

" I can't afford to fall. Let me have ahold of your collar. That groundhog hole is still out there waiting to break a brittle bone. The hole is all that's left after Carl wiped out a whole family of the varmints."

Cat cuts me a Catahoula look and says, "How is Mr. Carl these days?"

"Best farm overseer we've ever had. He controls the deer, wild turkey, raccoon, and polecat population. The squirrels and bunny rabbits don't take unnecessary chances. "

"They all have mothers too," says Cat.

"Right. And so do bats and bumblebees."

"Nuff said. Hang on to your dogwood walking stick your old buddy Merle

carved for you, and while you're at it, see if you can keep from choking me when you grab the collar. Damn dog collars anyway, especially choke collars. Sorry human invention. Oughta be outlawed."

"Collarless dogs can't be completely trusted."

"The hell you say, but let's not fuss. Wouldn't want you to mess up your eightieth birthday with a broken hip on top of everything else. Heard any coyotes lately?"

"About every night—usually about two a.m. when I get up to pee, they do their infernal non-stop yipping."

"Looking for easy food for their children. How's 'bout coydogs. Seen any of them?"

"No."

"Cross a coyote with a dog, you know what you got."

"Got one bloodthirsty menace."

"Make you and me stay on our toes," says Cat. "So let's you and me keep our eyeballs peeled, want to?"

Cat and I pick our steps as carefully as we dare. When we reach the back porch I look at the thermometer—"zero."

"O.K. Boss, now I want you to close your eyes, and keep 'em closed until we're well inside with Miz Scarlett. I want you to tell her to close her eyes too."

"All right, just don't let me fall."

"Don't be paranoid about the falling thing, Boss. You're doin' just fine. If you go down so do I, and I don't want any of my own ribs broken or worse. Humans have a bad habit of thinking we dogs live happy, dogdom lives no matter what happens to us—choke collars, muzzles, even in some cases three legs instead of four. Whatever it is, they call it a dog's life. What hog poop."

"Miz Scarlett," I say to my sweet wife, "we have a visitor, and she wants you to close your eyes."

"She what?"

"Cat has returned."

"I know. I told her where you were. Oh, mercy. Oh, thank the Lord. Oh, Cat, let me kiss your sweet face again. I knew you'd come back one day."

"Eyes closed?" I say to the Cat kisser.

"Closed."

"Mine too."

I take Miz Scarlett by her hand and with Cat leading the way we proceed past the Buck Stove beneath the portrait of my teenage mother in the warm-as-toast bedroom to the colder parlor, where all of a sudden, I never heard such a chorus of dogs:

"Happy Birthday to you, happy birthday to you, happy birthday dear Bosssss, happy birthday to you!"

"O.K., you can tell her she can open her eyes now, and you can open yours," says Cat as joyfully as if she'd taken hold of a wild hog's hairy ear.

"Where in the world did all these dogs come from?" I gasp.

"What dogs?" says a patient but bewildered Miz Scarlet, looking around what to her is a cold, uninhabited parlor.

"Boss, tell her they're all the dogs of your and her past, and I've arranged for them to be here in spirit on this glorious day in another February to wish you happy eightieth birthday, the happiest of eightieth birthdays. The very happiest!"

"We got ourselves a roomful of dogs, Miz Scarlett. Ain't that just a whopping good show?"

"Dogs? What dogs?" says Miz Scarlett. "I don't see any dogs!"

While she loves Cat as much as I do, my dearly beloved does not yet hear dog-talk much less see visiting spirit dogs. Right now, she's just a shade this side of paranoid. But with luck that might change. Cat and I will see if we can open wider her vision and persuade her that she too can go to the dogs without fear of any kind.

"I think I'm losin' it, but I'll go along with you. Proceed," she says warily.

As if by magic wand, Cat has mustered a whole cadre of dogs, including the first one in my life, Dusty, a beautiful cocker creature who used to sleep with me when I was a teenager. We'd stay warm together on stone-cold winter nights.

Dusty was a golden honey color with fine feathers on his legs. He was the companion I felt I so desperately needed, and we became inseparable from the moment I cupped him in my hands.

"My God, Dusty, how many years has it been?" I say as I gather him into my

21

arms one more time.

"About sixty-four. You went with your mother to live with your grandmother after your callow, starry-eyed doctor father passed on. I was brought in after the divorce from your no-nonsense stepfather. I was to fill a crying gap, so to speak."

"Gap?"

"You know, rhymes with 'yap'," chortles Cat.

The dogs laugh up a storm, but I don't think it's so funny.

Miz Scarlett shakes her head and sits down with a cup of chicory-flavored coffee from New Orleans, where she was born sixty-four years ago. She's spent the last twenty-four years putting up with Thurberian craziness on Plum Lick in Bourbon County, Kentucky. Every once in a while she yearns for Bourbon Street, the Old Absinthe House, and a streetcar named Desire, but none is presently in sight. Nor will be since the orchiectomy. On this day, just a parlor full of dogs wagging their tails off and scratching at angel fleas.

"Dusty, I'm sorry."

"About what?"

"You know. I didn't stop you from chasing cars. I may even have thought it was cute. Even urged you on."

"It's O.K. I'm having a glorious time chasing heavenly bitches. They're really a challenge."

"Old Tom dug your grave out by Grandmother's little outhouse, and I turned away and didn't look back when he shoveled in the dirt. After I cried, I went to see the man who had hit you, and I asked him if he had done it. He said, 'Yes, what are you going to do about it?' He was bigger and older than I was, and I thought there was nothing

23

else to do, so I turned and walked away. A cowardly thing."

"You're forgiven. Besides, chasing cars is something you learn to crave, and most of us dogs eventually pay dearly for the thrill of it."

"Darling, you 'member that three-legged dog in Mississippi?" I ask, as I add firewood to the parlor Buck Stove beneath the portrait of sternly-pinched great-grandmother Cynthia, a nine-teenth-century Plum Licker. She had a right to sing the outhouse blues, busy as she was having eight children and sur-viving another cholera epidemic.

"Paper Truck?"

"He's here," says Cat. "I brought him along because he's been asking about you, Miz Scarlett."

What once was the ghostly appearance of Paper Truck begins to take physical shape. The dogs blink in anticipation that Miz Scarlett is now not only hearing their voices but seeing each pointed or drooping ear, each eagerly wagging tail.

She sits back on the sofa and looks in amazement past her morning's first cup of coffee . "Darling Boy, you and Cat have done it. Paper Truck and friends have come back. I see them *all*."

"Paper Truck," I say, "you do remember Miz Scarlett when she was just a flower reaching for the sun from her mama's front porch in Woodville, Mississippi?"

"Sure do. Here's looking at you, Sweet Thing," he says, looking moon-eyed as he sidles up next to the sofa."

Miz Scarlett smiles wickedly.

"How did you get your name, Paper Truck?" I want to know.

"Thought you'd never ask. I had a thing about chasing paper trucks, big ones. Some people know them as Mississippi log trucks, the kind with the long, stripped trees hanging out the back. I went after one too many. Cost me a leg. Honestly earned me the name Paper Truck.

"Everybody respected you," croons Miz Scarlett.

"Except, I guess, the driver of the paper truck, who was too busy chewing on his Moon Pie."

"Probably didn't look back once on the way to the mill where they turn tall trees into toilet paper," says Miz Scarlett.

"Some folks loved me. I was what you would call the community dog—belonged to nobody."

"Guess you could say it pays to get outta the way of a paper truck when you see one bumpin' down the road."

"As for me and the love department during the gettin' on days, takes mighty real skill to muscle aside all the four-legged rapscallion brothers."

"That's life," says Miz Scarlett.

"Sweetheart," I say. "Thank God, you do have the ability to understand dog-speak. I knew you eventually would."

"Part of the caregiver's job," says Miz Scarlett.

"Yes, and here we are blessed with a room full of dogs from our pasts, and they've come a long way to wish me a happy eightieth birthday, and I'm right grateful. The least we can do is to make them welcome. Surely you can see them now as well as any southern belle can see tomorrow's best dream."

"Let the good dogs roll," she laughs.

"You could go chase a paper truck," I retort.

"Easy Boss," says Cat, "You've got one hellava good wife, no Blanche DuBois, and you ought to be thankful for her, especially for her gumbo and pecan pie."

"You're right. O.K.," I respectfully say. "Who's next?"

"I'm here!"

"Moby!"

I was on the young side of thirty, when I again felt the need to have a cocker spaniel member of the family, an unde-manding presence to help soften the blows of local radio and television re-porting. But why a cocker spaniel? I'm not sure. Maybe it was the unthreatening eyes and the memory of the earlier days of Dusty.

"Aye aye," says Moby ambling up with sleek under-slung lower jaw.

"You had a good, long life dodging all shapes and sizes of childhood spears, didn't you now?"

"Yep, I did. But remember, you gave me away just like Cat—forty-three years ago, when you left for the big time of

CBS in Washington, D.C. I was determined not to be left behind. Not then, not ever again.

"I found my way along who knows how many miles of evening rush-hour traffic on Brownsboro Road in Louisville, resisted every temptation to bite a single tire, showed up back on your doorstep across town, grateful to be home again."

"I'm ashamed."

"Don't need to be. And it ain't your fault that I almost immediately went blind in the nation's capital. Wouldn't be the first time it's happened up there."

"Constitutional debates?"

"Cataracts. Got me before the next move to Atlanta. Had sense enough to stay close to the back door, lived out my life in the dark until there was nothing to do but to be sent away to dog Heaven. Safer politicking up there. It was your late first wife, Rose, who fed me and brushed me until she finally had to take me to the last vet's visit."

"Excuse me," says Miz Scarlett as she rises. "I'll need more than one cup of coffee if this is going to go on as long as I think it is."

"Tell her to put another log on the fire," says Cat.

"Would you put another log on the fire, Sweet Thing?"

"I heard. And when I return from the outhouse I'll have kisses and hugs all around. Nothing like retreating to a three-holer when faced with a parlor full of imaginary dogs."

"Nothing like a Catahoula to get up a Mardi Gras crowd," says Cat. "You know you love us all."

"Yes, I do. And if it'll make you and your Boss happy, I'm taking this big leap of faith—your dogs are my dogs, your outhouse is my outhouse, your blues are my blues. So, throw me sumthin, Mistah!"

"By all the saints that go marchin' in, Boss, I think we've done it. Miz Scarlett not only hears us now, but she can really see us too.

While she's out of the parlor, Dirk the German shepherd is restless. Dirk was taken from a litter on sale at a Salt Lick reunion at a time when we judged we needed a little extra protective presence in and around our 1850 house. A little of the old "Who the hell are you?" kind of thing. "If you're looking for an easy fix this ain't the place. If you're up to no good I'll give you about two seconds to go on down the road."

"Why are you sniffing the legs of the piano, Dirk?"

"Can't help it."

"For God's sake, Dirk, don't raise your leg on Miz Scarlett's Kurtzmann Cabinet Grand. I mean, don't even think about it."

"Checking for drugs. Remember, you sent me off to become a drug dog—once a drug dog, always a drug dog. Let's see what we might have here. Never can be too sure. Have to check. Fancy Cabinet Grands don't mean a thing to me. It's what's inside the music that matters. When was the last time you and she puffed a little love tune here?"

"I can save you the trouble. We don't do drugs. And you know damn well we don't. And I repeat, do *not* pee on Miz Scarlett's piano leg. As a matter of fact, don't pee on anything in this house. She'll clean your drug-sniffing clock if you do.

"That goes for all you other dogs too."

"I'm done," says Dirk. "You're clean."

"May I have a word here?" asks Chief, the rottweiler, from the back of the gathering.

"Certainly you may," say I.

It was Chief who replaced Dirk. Chief had big feet and the usual two dollops of tan above the eyes on the fierce face, like roaming, unshakeable headlights in a dark tunnel.

"You know, I had thought I would fit in here. But it was the silly sheep that were my undoing."

"All you had to do was to curb your appetite for lamb."

"I know. And I'll never forget the day you took one of the lambs I'd killed and tied it around my neck. Made me wear it like it was a John Wayne bandanna. That was pretty rough."

"Imagine how the lamb felt."

"I understand. But if it was all right for you and Miz Scarlett to dine on lamb medium-well with mint, I figured it was O.K. for me to taste it rare right off the hoof. Like some of the others here today, I was sent down the road."

"You were happy with your new home?"

"Sure was. My new boss didn't waste time with sheep. He knew most of the filthy wool didn't pay the shearing bill. Duhhh! So I developed a taste for rocks. I'd bring them from the creek to the house and pile them up as neat as you please. Nobody had a problem with that. Matter of fact, they bragged on me about it. And they never once tied a rock around my neck."

"I'm back," says Miz Scarlett, giving well-undeserved kisses to me and Cat. She blows kisses to each of the other dogs awaiting her return. "Now then," she sighs, settling back again into the puffy French Quarter pillows.

"Speaking as your ever ready voodoo lady, I'm delighted to see all these dogs in our parlor situated on Plum Lick Creek, where the water rolls down to New Orleans. Born as I was on the Ides of March in the Crescent City of dreams, here's to all the hurricane toasts at Pat O'Brien's. I raise the noble glass to each of you dogs gathered here today in honor of Boss on his eightieth birthday. I am delighted that I can join in your revelry, because I hear and see each of you as clearly as a full moon over Lake Pontchartrain."

"Well, let's see. I declare, Cat, you may have to help an old feist in the breeze of this surprise birthday party and, moreover, the celebration of Miz Scarlett's coming out. Please make the rest of the introductions."

"Gladly,"says Cat. "Here're Chip and NCAA (Nee-ka), the border collies; Pumpkin and Muddy River, the Australian shepherds; we've already been reunited with Chief, the rottweiler, and Dirk, the German shepherd; which leaves us with Kink, the orphan Lab/chow mix; Turkey, the dachshund; Ewedawg and Lambdawg, the Great Pyrenees; and Zoee's Patricia O'Casey, the Irish setter."

"Good Lord, Pat," I say. "I'll never forget that Father's Day on Flowerdale Lane in Dallas, Texas, when you birthed *fifteen* squirming Irish setters."

"Tell me all about it," says Pat as she sprawls before the fire. I'll not forget it either, even though it was thirty years ago."

"Good grief, Pat," says Miz Scarlett.

"You bring back memories of Columbus, Ohio, where Boss and I were married by a judge in the middle of a mammoth blizzard. You went to Kentucky while we dealt with other kinds of storms in South America—Jonestown among them. As soon as that monster year was over, we were reunited at Uncle Jimmy's house on Navarre Street in New Orleans. We were determined that there had to be more than one Zoee's Patricia O'Casey, and you were well bred in Dallas, when CBS moved us there."

Pat groans and rolls her eyes. "Let me tell you, I'll never forget two hundred and seventy needle-sharp claws working inside me, and that doesn't count thirty dewclaws and thirty eye buds, either, let me tell you, Miz Scarlett."

"Wonder where all the little wigglies are today?" says Cat.

"Wherever they are," says Pat, "I hope

the little darlings don't show up again anytime soon, if ever. Imagine being nearly nippled to death by the spiky little teeth of Rosebud, Duke, Beauregard, Scarlett O'Hara, Rebel, Rhett, Casey, Heidi, Gen. Robert E. Lee, Shamrock, Jefferson Davis, Shawn, Davy Crockett, William Stamps, and, for God's dog's sake—Dallas. May all my fifteen children rest in peace some place else. They must be, 'cause I haven't seen 'em in my corner of Heaven, yet.

"I should like to make a public apology," says Cat. "I should like to ask forgiveness from Pumpkin and Kink."

"Oh, really," says black-as-night Kink with the crook in his tail. "This oughta be good."

"Why, yes," says Pumpkin. "But how would you of all dogs have the fang to ask for forgiveness for anything?"

"I'm sorry for all the times, Kink, when I went for your soft underside, grabbed your right leg and flipped you bottom-up. But I will say I was not responsible for that permanent 90-degree angle in the last eight inches of your tail. You showed up that way after having been dumped out on the farm road. And whose fault was that? Miz Scarlett called you Kinky."

"Kinky my butt. Let me tell you sumthin'. I got mighty wore out with those insulting flips, flops, and ear nibblins, and I went on down the road to live out my life without any Catahoulas in it. I wasn't ashamed to be a crooked-tailed orphan again and that's a dog-damned fact."

"Pumpkin, I'm sorry…"

"Yeah, you're sorry about all the times when I was standing there on a full stomach, and you hit me broadside like a screaming cannonball…sent me and all my gray and white feathers winding into Miz Scarlett's flower garden."

"I'm troubled."

"Troubled? Boss brought you in here, the good Lord knows why, and right away you had to play the territory card. Let me tell you sumthin', Miz Kat-can-du: We dogs with roots in Australia have class and character you Catahoulas never once dreamed of. So give us a break."

"All right. I've sincerely asked for your forgiveness. Will you be so kind as to favor me with it? Or do I have to whip

41

up on you one more time?"

"I'll speak to St. Peter about it," says Pumpkin. "He'll grab *you* by the ear. Boss, I want to tell you and your beloved that when I disappeared from Plum Lick that day long ago, it was with the heaviest of hearts."

"Miz Scarlett, do you hear Pumpkin?"

"I wish I didn't have to."

"I went down Plum Lick Creek and let the coyotes have me. They really worked me over, fighting for my liver. See, I was growing older, just like you good people. One day you'll have to take the long walk, too. And the coyotes will be yippin' and waitin' for *you*. Not a good way to die, but the outcome has been blessed."

"Miz Scarlett, Pumpkin wants us to understand that she left us because Cat drove her off."

"I know. Pumpkin, bless you. There's never been a day or night that I've not

thought of you and wished you were back here so I could again hold your face against mine. Right before you disappeared, I remember getting down on my knees in front of you as you were sitting in the cool of the back porch. I held your face between my hands, leaned in and whispered in your ear, 'I love you.' And I still do."

"Thank you, Miz Scarlett. That's all I needed to hear."

"Sweetheart, you are truly hearing this parlor full of dogs?" I say with a trifle of doubt.

"'If you can't lick 'em, join 'em,' my Deep South mama and daddy used to say. I took their advice all the way to New York City, and it worked wonders on cab drivers."

"But, how come the South lost the wah?" asks Cat with waving battle flags in her eyes.

"I wouldn't go there," say I.

"Wasn't it because Johnny Rebs were usually late showing up for battles or almost anything, except maybe to write letters to magnolia-waving girlfriends and their adoring, dug-in mamas and daddies paddling their pirogues in the coonass bayous?"

"Cat," says Miz Scarlett, "that's about enough ungrateful, sassy Yankee lip, and I don't want to hear one more word about what was a horribly tragic time."

"Well now," says Cat, "this is a fine day, indeed. Pumpkin and Kink have forgiven me after a fashion, Boss has turned eighty, and Miz Scarlett has entered the world of United States of America dogspeak!"

"Don't see why not. But that doesn't mean I'm ready to whistle Dixie, so you can forget that," she sniffs.

"Well now," says Cat. "Since you finally can hear me, let me ask you, Miz Scarlett, if you see anybody here you remember besides Paper Truck."

"Hot damn, Git Down!"

"Right here, Miz Scarlett."

"Lord have mercy. Come here and let me just say, git up here in my lap like you always wanted to and stay as long as you want to. Never thought I'd see you again!"

"Here I come!"

Git Down lands in Miz Scarlett's lap in a tangle of four skinny black legs and three white stockings.

"Last time I saw you, you were wearin' a red bandanna around your neck and truckin' on down the road to the new place you'd adopted. 'Member when you ate half the couch in that miserable little 8' x 36' tin trailer we rented and called home? You shat foam rubber for four days. Served you right," says Miz Scarlett giving her wandering vagabond dog a squeeze.

"Anybody else?" asks Cat.

"Well, let's see. There were…Patsy…Dixie…Rosie…and Socks. But wait a minute, where's Duff?" she wants to know as she scans the canine cadre.

"I'm here! Do you think you might tell Git Down to git down so I can have some lap time? Help me up, Miz Scarlett, because I've turned eighty-four. Can't jump up the way I used to. But I'll say this, going up to Northern Kentucky to live with your youngest daughter, Ravy, has been very good. She and her new husband, John, look after me real well in these miniature poodle clearing-the-deck times."

"I'll always remember how tiny and frightened you seemed that first day in the animal-shelter cage. I picked you up and said, 'You're going home with us.' Didn't look like a poodle at all! More like a shaved white rat with a fluffy head and tail."

"Although I'd not yet learned to talk—I was only five months old—I felt the warmth of the palm of your hand, and I knew it was possible that I could be loved. I vowed never to disappoint you, or Ravy when she was struggling with high school and those turbulent college years."

"O.K., guys," says Cat. "Time for a pee break—males to the water maples, females to the sleeping jonquils."

"You pee on those jonquils and there'll be Hell to pay," says Miz Scarlett.

"While they're outside, Darling," say I, "Tell me, how do you account for your sudden ability to communicate with dogs?"

"Because I love you. I suppose it was Pumpkin's story that truly connected. Why didn't we take better care of her in her last years?"

"I regret that very much. I have no explanation."

"When Pumpkin and the others come back in, I'd like to have a word with the true-blue southern rebels—Dixie, Patsy, Rosebud, and Socks—assuming they're here. Do you think they might be?" asks the waddling child from New Orleans who grew up to become the Revlon beauty from Mississippi.

"Miz Scarlett," says Cat, after bounding in from the snow-rimmed front porch, "gotcha covered. I was going to surprise you, save the best for last so to speak."

"Talk to me."

"Well, here's Dixie."

"For goodness sake!"

Dixie, the Pomeranian-dachshund, leaps into Miz Scarlett's arms, and they like to not quit kissing.

"Oh, Dixie, you didn't belong to me...I belonged to you."

"You saved me from that hideous dog pound in Houston, Texas, but then you gave me up when you moved to Columbus, Ohio. Was your career with Revlon all that important?"

"I thought it was at the time. Yes, I did. And I'm sorry."

"It's O.K."

"You went everywhere with me. Remember? I was traveling in south Texas on the way to the Rio Grande. U.S. 77 went right through the King Ranch— no stations, no towns. Had to pull in to a rest stop. No bathroom facility for me. You bounced out of the car, through the fence, never mind the sign that said,

'Beware of Rattlesnakes.' I said, 'Dixie, y'all on your own. I'm going to wait here until you come back, if ever you do.'"

"I did. But you sent me to live with one of your friends in Mississippi, which was all right until I picked a fight with a hub cap out on the Centreville Road along where the pine trees reach for the sky."

"All right," says Cat, "cut the tears. Here're Patsy and Betty, the Boston terriers from New Orleans, when you were still in babyhood, Miz Scarlett. They say they pulled you in the carriage on the banquette on Fountainbleu Drive on special days back in the late forties. You might say they were your steeds, you their Cinderella-in-waiting."

"Come here, darling girls. Let me hold you one more time. Make room, Dixie."

"Your mama was Eulalie, so you became Little Lalie. That was what they called you then," says Patsy. "We don't know about this Miz Scarlett business. You remember the garbage wagon pulled by that old sway-back horse? I'd hear the clompity clomp of the nag and would start running like crazy through the house."

"And I, dressed in saggy diapers running right behind you? Squealing the whole way to the porch," laughs Miz Scarlett.

"Usually the screen door was latched," says Patsy, "and I stood there quivering and raging like a caged tiger. One day, somebody forgot to close the latch. I hit the screen, it banged open, and I was propelled like a bird in the direction of the garbage wagon. Landed—plop— right beneath the head of the horse. It was said when I looked up at the kind old nag that I had a wide-as-you-please grin on my face! Maybe the horseflesh smiled back. I'm not sure. But after that, I always checked the screen door latch to make sure it was fastened. Then, and only then, did I rage."

"I wasn't there at the time," says Betty, "but I can tell you she's been raging ever since!"

The years ripped, raged, and roared by.

"And then there's Rosie," says Miz Scarlett reaching down and lifting her little old friend to her lap. "I was living in Delhi, Louisiana, and it was a cold night. I was visiting at a friend's house where they were building Interstate 20. A lot of people were dumping dogs out, left and right. I had just arrived at the house and behind me like a streak of lighting came this little bitty shivering dog, looked like a cross between a Chihuahua and a Manchester terrier. My heart melted. I dubbed her 'Rosebud.'

"She was my constant companion, and she would come home with me on weekends to Mississippi. My father was charmed by this little pup not much bigger than a squirrel. She was delicate, dainty, not a yappy dog. She was a lady.

"The February day that my father died he'd been sitting on the side of the bed, elbows braced on his knees, and he was holding his head with the palms of his hands. An hour before, Rosebud had come into the bedroom, came and sat right between Daddy's feet and looked up at him. He said, 'That is one sweet little dog.' She must've known that something was bad wrong.

"I thank you, Rosie."

"I only wish I could have saved him."

"Rosie Two was the second little dog I got in Houston, because the first Rosie became my mother's companion after

Daddy died. I just had to replace her when Rosie went to Heaven. At the shelter there was one big cage, and one little brown dog in it. I picked up a piece of identifying paper. Can you believe t? The name of the dog was actually Rosebud! I sobbed for twenty minutes. It was a sign from Rosie One above, and needless to say, Rosie Two was taken to Woodville."

"Thank you, Miz Scarlett," says Rosie Two, "and bless you, your mama Eulalie, and your papa Charlie.

"And then there is Socks. Poor Socks. Come here, sweetie," says Miz Scarlett as she pats the sofa beside her.

"Socks was a donation from Brother Waites, minister and educator in southern Mississippi. Socks was looking for a permanent home, sort of. So what if she is short, brown, and ugly with a white muzzle. Socks couldn't help it, could you, Socks? Socks was an 'it.' She was also a magnet for fleas, but she knew how to do her civic duty. She'd jump into the town patrol car and make the rounds with the policeman on night shift. She finally disappeared in Baton Rouge when Mama was staying with sister Cornelia for a spell."

"I tried to get back to your mama, Miz Scarlett, but it wasn't meant to be, I suppose. I know you all did your best to find me, and I know your mama suffered deeply. I wish it could have been different. All I know is, for me the lights went out in Baton Rouge."

"Oh, my gosh," exclaims Miz Scarlett. "It's been over fifty years since I've seen you two, Snow and Flake. Snow was one of my father's bird dogs. He was totally white and loved to put those quail on point. Stud service was offered. The pick of the litter was Flake. You sure lived up to your name, honey. You were absolutely nuts. You too were hit by a car, and my sisters and I cried like babies. Snow had a bad kidney ailment. Died of it, and we cried all over again. We sure loved you both."

"All God's dogs got problems," says Cat, rolling her steely, ice-blue Catahoula eyes in the direction of Snow and Flake.

"Thurber wrote, 'If I have any beliefs about immortality, it is that certain dogs I have known will go to Heaven, and very few persons.'

"Does this not include Snow and Flake?" I ask.

"Hear, hear," says Cat.

"Well," say I, "this party can't go on much longer. But, I too must ask forgiveness on my eightieth birthday. I mean to say, I too want to clear the decks as best I can."

"Turn loose and let 'er fly," says Cat.

"Well, Muddy River, I know it's probably asking too much, but I'm sorry about how I scared you so bad with the choke collar. I cut you no slack. I was trying to discipline you to come when called. You planted your feet and refused to follow commands."

"Let me just say this: There was something inside of me that deeply resented you coming on so strong on that hot day of summer. If you had just given me a chance to come to you first, in my own time, in my own way—I, a little ole Australian shepherd, one puny little Muddy River—it might all have been different."

"I see that now. I was wrong, and I'm sorry."

"It's all right. You're forgiven. Will you forgive me for being so stubborn?"

"I do. But, what ever happened to you?"

"I went over the hill, where on a full-moon night I was no match for the coyotes. They drew a circle that locked me in. I fought the good fight, but when it was all over I was one Bloody River."

"Well then, I need to get down on my knees and apologize to Ewedawg and Lambdawg."

"The tradition of the Great Pyrenees has been sadly damaged by what was endured here," says Ewedawg with a shake of her enormous, white, shaggy head. "You brought me here as a pup and expected me to guard your stinky sheep, defend them with my very life."

"Yes, I did."

"Well, I roughed up that stupid little lamb, might even have killed it, because I hardly knew the difference between a baby sheep and a ball of yarn to be played with. So you brought in Lambdawg to teach me a thing or two. This bigger-than-bejesus Great Pyrenees mama went after me like I was Satan herself. When it was all over there was nothing to do but get the Hell out of Dodge. Miles away, somewhere on a distant hillside, I heard what must have been a shotgun explosion. Day turned into night. Just like that. Like snapping a dewclaw, if you had one. I must've been considered a threat by somebody. I paid for mine, didn't I?"

The painful recounting of a sad time from the dogs' perspective brings back memories of what I wrote in my first book, *The View from Plum Lick.*

> *I had come to the knowledge that responsibility for a dog's life begins at or very near birth and continues without interruption to that final moment of*

truth. I knew taking a dog to the vet to be put down had become an accepted practice in the United States, as it had in many other parts of the 'civilized' world, but I now viewed it as a cop-out, especially when handling working dogs on the farm. They are animals in the same way cattle, hogs, and sheep are animals. Working dogs have a function to perform, and they are bred for that one thing. A Great Pyrenees snoring away in front of a living room fire becomes a sad sight.

While Ewedawg had gotten off on the wrong paw, her older half-sister, Lambdawg, had never laid one of her massive, white-furred paws on defenseless sheep, young or old. In fact, her previous owner said, when a lamb had recently died of natural causes, and the frail little body was tossed to the other side of the fence, Lambdawg went over there, lay down, curled her body around

the lifeless form and tried to comfort it as
if it were her own.

Ewedawg was still at the vet's office in
town; the decision had been to spare but
spay her. In a few days she'd be back on
the farm. When she returned, she'd have
Lambdawg as her probation officer. We
had no guarantee it was going to work,
but we figured it would be worth a try.

"Lambdawg, it was all up to you."

"I took charge the instant I laid eyes on Ewedawg, and my message was as clear as a sharp bark on a 40-below-zero night: 'Get out of town. Don't come back. Ever.'"

"After you had the whole show to yourself, Lambdawg, you began to roam. No matter what we tried, you couldn't be kept anywhere near home. You were tied to tires, and you dragged the heavy rubber to Kingdom Come. You were tied to fence posts, and you broke free."

"Any smart shepherd should have re-membered what he'd been told," says Lambdawg. "It's almost impossible to imprison a Great Pyrenees. Our concept of territory does not conform to a human's. Boundaries become silly—im-possible to enforce."

"On an especially hot day, you had been tied to a corner post in the back lot.

Upon the return home, it was easy to tell from as far away as the barn, there was something wrong.

"Maybe you were asleep," I thought.

"I was asleep all right."

"You were dead."

"I had become ensnared in the fence."

There's a hush, then a moan in the parlor. Miz Scarlett puts a kerchief to her eyes. The dogs blink. My feeling of guilt burns deep inside me. I remember unfastening the leather collar, Lambdawg's fine head falling softly to the ground beneath the shade of the giant sycamore, the flock of sheep staring.

"There was nothing to do but return to the house and come back with the Ford pickup with the rusty tailgate. I backed it close to your long, limp body, Lambdawg, and closed the tailgate so you wouldn't fall out."

"We went over the hill together, didn't

we?" says Lambdawg.

"Yes. I parked the truck near a grove of locust trees, opened the tailgate and rolled you over the end of it. I dragged you inside the grove, then turned and walked away."

"Nothing to mark the spot?" asks Lambdawg.

"No. Nothing at all," I say. "It was a day of shame."

"And you are for- given," says Lambdawg, gently placing a paw on my knee.

"Ewedawg and I have be- come friends. We do the best we can to watch out for heavenly sheep. When you join us there, I think there may be work for you as a better kind of shepherd."

"A little shepherd of Kingdom Come," says Cat.

"Hear, hear!" says Miz Scarlett.

"Whooom have we missed?" asks Cat. "Let's see. There are Chip and NCAA (AKA Nee-ka). You had a murderous thing about cats whatever their stripes, whatever their furtive strategies, didn't you? Or, so I've been told."

"Sure did," says half-breed Border collie Nee-ka. "Hated all kinds of cats. They knew I meant business. If I could grab them by the scruff of the neck I would do just that, and the old slam-dunk fest would be a done deal, so to speak. I could have been a national champion."

"What became of you?"

"Remember the day I was accused of killing sheep?"

"You were lucky to be spared."

"That whine of the bullet got my attention, and I too got out of Dodge. I've been warned that we're to leave cats alone in Heaven, and I'll tell you, it's one great big temptation."

"Chip," I say, "you may have a word or two, but before you do, we need to honor a very special little dog, a small standard dachshund whose name is—ta da—Turkey!"

With a gleeful run, threading his way among the bigger dogs, Turkey proves that his short, stubby gait across the bare poplar floor can still sound like a whole kennel of dogs.

"You were a 1985 Thanksgiving present for Miz Scarlett. I brought you to the dining room table and presented you to her as if you were truly the guest of honor, newest member of the family that for better or worse has embraced so many dogs. We played Name That Dog, and in honor of the day and the noble bird, 'Turkey' was the logical choice."

"Oh my," says Miz Scarlett as she covers her face with her hands. "We are so sorry about what happened that following summer of drought on Plum Lick. Wish it had never been."

"Yes, Ma'am," says Turkey. "On that scorching hot day Chip and I were looking for a taste of water, and I thought we'd found a little pleasure in the concrete watering trough up above bone-dry Plum Lick Creek. Chip was tall enough to stand up close to the tank to reach in to get a drink, but since I was so short I had to jump, and—well, I landed inside the tank and couldn't get out. You might say I was stuffed and slow-cooked right then and there."

"Turkey," cries Miz Scarlett, "I should never have left you out of the house to run with the other dogs. You were so special to me. Can you ever forgive me?"

"You know I do. Up in Heaven we spend our days forgiving one another."

"Chip, you were every shepherd's dream," I say.

"I tried, but I couldn't save Turkey.

"You were a purebred Border collie whose passion was to gather the sheep and put them where I wanted them. Simple as that."

"I never wanted to disappoint you, Boss. As for the sheep, they needed somebody to show them the way and keep them from doing something really 'tupid."

"Yes, and for that we had Lady, the Yugoslavian guard dog. Is she here?"

"Yes."

"Where?"

"Over here"

"I see you way over in that corner.

Come out where we all can see you,"
says Miz Scarlett.

"You know, I never was much on talking."

"Still dogs run deep."

"I distrusted all human beings, even
those who fed me."

"How well I remember. But Miz
Scarlett and I admired you greatly. We'd
set out your pan of food, and then we'd
walk away. Only then would you come
to it. We'd look back, but that's all."

"Lady," says Miz Scarlett, "I'll always
remember the day after the last of the
flock of sheep was sold, Chip was sent
away, and there was nothing left for you
to do. After a week, you seemed so lonely."

"I was."

"Pretty soon you came into the yard,
hollowed out a place to lie, and watched
every move we made outside. You were
guarding us!"

"We found a new home for you with

Frank and Annie in Montgomery
County. He was a vet, and she a breeder
of fine wool-producing sheep."

"Good people."

"But how were we going to catch you?
That was the question."

"Tranquilizers didn't work even though
you shot me with enough to kill a calf."

"There was a thunderstorm one night,"
I say, "and we found you in the corner of
one of the deserted barn stalls."

"Didn't know where else to go."

"I slipped the leather muzzle on you and led you out," I recall.

"I wasn't going to bite you."

"I didn't get it in writing."

"Real funny," says Cat.

"Well, we took you over to Frank and Annie's, and you stayed there for the rest of your life, faithfully guarding their sheep. They said you dug a hole in the pasture and hid there like a submarine with the scope always up. Coyotes never understood how you always knew where they were."

"Stayed out of Dodge, didn't they?"

"Well, old age finally caught up with you, and Frank had to put you down."

"So now," says Lady, "I've found my voice in Heaven."

"Any coyotes or coydogs up there?"

"Sure. But the Good Dog Lord sees to it that all critters behave."

"Alligators and rattlesnakes too?"
"We don't push our luck."

"All right, children. You're pushing your luck with me," says Miz Scarlett. "Since I assume you're not staying for warmed-up dog biscuits, why don't we say goodbye until, say, 2020, when Boss hopes to be ninety years old?"

"Sounds real good," says Cat.

"Then the big one will be 2030 when I reach the great big ole sunset of one hundred," say I with a smile for Miz Scarlett.

"Only if the outhouse will still be open to sing the blues in," Cat chortles.

"The outhouse will always be available to friends and strangers alike if I have anything to say about it," I say with a tear looking for a way down my wrinkled cheek. "Might even include a small bottle of white lightning within easy reach if we play our dewclaws right."

"Could we leave out the centerfold?" asks Miz Scarlett.

"How 'bout that, Boss?" Cat smiles.

"Why sure. But all dreams are approved in advance."

"O.K. guys," says Cat, "Let's hear it one more time for Boss and Miz Scarlett. Key of C. All together now!"

> For they're jolly good fellows,
> For they're jolly good fellows,
> For they're jolly good fellows,
>   That no dog can deny!

"O.K. Boss," says Cat. "Or shall I say, 'Jolly Good Fellow'?"

"Call me what you will, but be sure to call me for the supper bowl."

"Is there something you'd like to tell us all—some Plum Lick sage advice about yourself, about cancer, about the outhouse, about the world as it is, and as it perhaps is to become?"

"Let me think."

"Take all the time you need, but Miz Scarlett's pushin' us to the door and your friends must soon be on their way Home."

"First of all, never, never, never give up. And moreover, I should like to use the words of Peter Pence, a hundred-year-old hermit with whom I had a conversation many years ago."

"The floor is yours."

"Since I am human, body-bound like all of us, I have cells of earthbound limitations."

"Does this philosophy include dogs?"

"Don't interrupt."

"Sorry."

"I believe we all have a soul, and I believe that it both lives in these mortal, aging bags of bones and will live forever outside what we presently see and feel."

"Listen up, critters," Cat commands as some of the dogs shift about on their haunches.

"I believe I have an earthly responsibility to marry good deeds with good faith and submit myself to God's judgment as to whether in His eyes it's good enough for me to be welcomed in His Home. That ought to pretty much sum it up."

"Miz Scarlett," says Cat, "Or may I say, Dawlin'?"

"Why sure, Honey."

"What else would you like to say to this body of lowly dogs assembled?"

"About what?"

"About home. About yourself. About Boss. About his shortening time. About the cancer that's gnawing on his bones."

"I have no idea how or when the Good Lord will call us home, but I'm going to enjoy every second of being together with Darling Boy as long as I can."

"Well said. And all of us dogs are going to be either down here or up there always pulling for you two to have the best part of each of these priceless moments," says Cat, with the Catahoula look blazing in her eyes.

"God bless you all," say I, "but I've got to get back to the outhouse."

"To sing some more blues?"

"Might toot one or two tunes."

"C'mon, God's dogs. Lets head on up the road," snaps Cat. "We have nothing to fear, ain't that right, Boss?"

"One more thing," say I.

"Hold on, dogs. I think Boss wants to send us off with some more stirring words for the next twenty years. Or is it twenty-five?"

"I like twenty-five if Miz Scarlett can put up with me and the outhouse doesn't float away."

"Right on," smiles Miz Scarlett with her grandest Garden District "well-come-right-on-in" radiance. "When you're one hundred and five, I'll be a lovely ninety, and we can talk and walk with the dogs toward the best sunset of all down where the waters of Plum Lick Creek and the Mississippi River head out to sea."

Cat pauses thoughtfully and asks, "What is life then?"

"Life is as big as the whole wide world and as precious as a single dewdrop," says Miz Scarlett.

"It's true," says Pumpkin. "An old cliché, but life is truly what you make it."

"What about aging?" Dixie wants to know. "Now there's a piece of secessional work."

"Our minds cannot be limited by the package in which they find themselves," says Miz Scarlett looking to the western side of the parlor to admire the portrait of her great-great grandfather Alexander, who left Kentucky to seek his fortune in New Orleans. He found it in mahogany, lost it in the War Between the States, and died of what was then called "softening of the brain."

"We didn't design the package, did we?" says Turkey. "The Great God Dog made some of us long and lowered us almost to the ground."

"Some of us He made glassy-eyed," says Cat.

"Tall for the occasion," chimes in Paper Truck.

"Some of us He made great swimmers," laughs Moby.

"Some of us He gave big hearts, and some of us he gave useless little dewclaws," says Zoee's Patricia O'Casey."

"It's what you've got in your head that matters and how you share it with others," says Miz Scarlett through her mother's embroidered kerchief.

"Attitude?" wonders Rosebud.

"Attitude is the essence of everything,"

replies Miz Scarlett.

"Ladies and gentlemen," says Cat, "Shall we go forward?"

"Hear, hear," chorus the dogs.

"All right," says Cat. "Let's head on up the road."

I stand there on the front porch with one hand gripping my dogwood walking stick, the other around Miz Scarlett. We watch the dogs pass out of sight across the big hill. I pull the most beautiful woman in the world in close and gave her a kiss to remember.

"Thank you, Lalie, for understanding."

"Understanding?"

"My need to talk to the dogs."

"Your need is my need."

I head back to the tabernacle.

As I sit myself down on the center throne, I remember magnificent Cat, her

wise resolve and steely determination,
the doctors and nurses who want me to
live, and Miz Scarlett's beauty and her
faithfully patient caregiving.

All of a sudden a very cold winter
seems far less forbidding, and I begin to
hum a sweeter, more promising outhouse
blues.